Old Ike

The Fictionalized Story of Woodrow Wilson's Ram

by Andrew Hager

The POTUS Pets Series, Book One

Written for the Presidential Pet Museum

DEDICATION

For the animals—presidential and otherwise—who improve our lives; and for my children, Ian and Mia.

CONTENTS

ACKNOWLEDGMENTS

I would like to thank my editor, Tricia Rogalski, for her regular input and encouragement. Without her, this project would never have gotten off the ground. Her saintly patience is matched only by her devilish humor.

Tristen Fagg read early drafts of this work and provided valuable feedback.

I have never raised sheep, and I was shockingly uninformed about them before undertaking this book. Special thanks, then, to Dr. Angela King, a chemistry professor at Wake Forest University, who has given her off-hours to sheep. She was generous enough to advise me, and it was she who told me you can never turn your back to a ram.

It also seems important to acknowledge all of my teachers who made learning history so much fun. The past is a collection of stories, after all, and when properly told, they are fascinating. Thank you to Joanna Bontrager, Carol Friend, Margaret Pegg, Edward Fearer, Dan Zack, and Joseph La Presta for the education.

This book would not have been possible without the support of the Director of the Presidential Pet Museum, Bill "WooFDriver" Helman. It was Bill's vision to begin this project and he trusted me completely.

Claire McLean's legwork as founder of the museum provided a foundation which made my research easier.

Nora Sawyer, through her keen artistic vision, brought Old Ike and his team of players to life on the page with her lively illustrations. I couldn't have asked for more.

Finally, my wife Kristy believed I could be a writer even more than I believed it. She held my nose to the grindstone and made sure I kept at it. Without her, I would have napped my way through this time and missed this opportunity.

1 THE NEW STAFF

The truck rumbled loudly onto the White House grounds. A groundskeeper directed the driver to pull onto the grass as other men moved to the rear of the truck. As the vehicle idled, the men opened the tailgate and peered in at the cargo.

"Is that what we've been waiting for, boss?" asked the younger man. The older man puffed idly on a cigar and nodded.

There were thirteen ewes milling around the truck bed, skittish from the long, bumpy drive over rutted, unpaved roads. They showed no desire to leave the truck. In fact, most of them pressed toward the back, away from the strangers who had opened the gate.

From the back of the herd, a single ram stepped forward, shoving aside his companions until he stood facing the men. The young groundskeeper took a step back, awed by the thick horns curling back over the ram's head. The boss stood his ground, exhaling a smoke ring that floated toward the ram and broke over his snout. The animal raised his head and inhaled deeply, his nostrils widening to take in the smell.

"He sure is an ugly brute," said the boss, turning to face his companion. "Reminds me of my old uncle Ike, who had a face even his mother couldn't love."

He doubled over, cackling at his own joke and the memory of his unfortunate uncle. The ram leaped from the truck's bed, lowering his head and driving it right into the laughing man's backside.

The man tumbled to the ground, no longer amused by the animal's appearance. He had dropped his cigar during his fall, and the ram was chewing on the unlit end as if the tobacco had been his goal the whole time. Now it was the younger man's turn to laugh.

"Looks like Old Ike got his revenge, doesn't it?" he chuckled.

"Be quiet," grumbled his boss, "and get those sheep off the truck."

***

Early the next morning, a gaggle of reporters gathered on the lawn to watch the sheep eat the grass. Old Ike, as the groundskeepers had taken to calling the ram, moved among the ewes but kept an eye on the crowd.

President Woodrow Wilson emerged from the White House, accompanied by his wife, Edith. He was a tall, thin man of sixty, dressed in a simple, dark gray suit, with round spectacles perched on his nose. He waved to the assembled press then motioned to the animals gobbling up his grass.

"Gentlemen," he said. "Meet the newest members of the White House staff! These magnificent beasts are part of this nation's war effort. Where once men were required to keep this building's grounds trim and neat, now these sheep shall do it."

He looked around at the crowd. "The men," he said, "have volunteered for the army and will soon be on their way to Europe!"

There was a polite round of applause from the reporters, who were trying to support their president now that the United States had entered the war, but there was a great deal of uncertainty among them.

The war in Europe had been going on for more than three years, with the British and French locked in a standstill with the Germans. Tens of millions of people in those countries had died so far, and there was no end to the hostilities in sight. How many American boys would die in foreign trenches before the fighting ended?

Wilson continued, explaining that the wool from his new animals would be auctioned off in support of the Red Cross, a relief organization that supported America's troops. There was more applause now, as the press considered how much money presidential wool might fetch on the auction block.

Old Ike stepped toward the president, posing nobly alongside the Commander-in-Chief.

"Consider this fine specimen," Wilson added. "Like our nation, he is quiet and strong. He keeps to himself, bothers no one. But when he is threatened—when danger looms near the herd—he acts decisively, using his strength for what is Right and True."

"Surely," a reporter called to the president, "our great country deserves a better-looking champion than that."

President Wilson cleared his throat, and he was about to chastise the reporter's rudeness when Old Ike charged the outspoken man. The press corps scattered as the ram advanced. The offending man was chased until he managed to jump a low hedge into another part of the grounds. Ike snorted, then began munching on the hedge, as if nothing had happened.

"You see, gentlemen?" the president asked, "This is how the United States responds to such indignities. We are a nation of action, a nation of will. Do not test us."

With that, he and his wife strode into the White House, leaving the reporters in Old Ike's care.

2 SACRIFICES

Around the time of Woodrow Wilson's presidency, the number of people who used tobacco products began to rise dramatically. People had been chewing and smoking tobacco for centuries, but now it could be processed in factories. Cigarettes and cigars were cheaper than ever. Advertisers began to promote smoking. Because the link between smoking and cancer was still unknown, few people worried that it would affect their health.

And so it was that Old Ike, the lone ram on the White House lawn, found plenty of cigar butts on the ground. Every time visitors gathered there, they threw their used tobacco products onto the lawn. The other sheep ignored them, but not Ike. Yes, he chewed the grass, but he saw no reason to pass over the delicious ashy remnants of half-smoked stogies. The tobacco released nicotine into his gums, and soon he was addicted.

The president did not smoke. Instead, he strolled the grounds with his wife Edith, and often they sat on wicker chairs to drink lemonade at sunset. They had been married little more than a year, and they were very much in love.

"Edith," the president would say, "we are fortunate."

"Yes," she would reply. "We certainly are."

Every conversation began that way. Then, they would discuss the events of the day—the bills currently before Congress, the news from Europe, who had visited the Oval Office that afternoon. The president shared everything with Edith.

Old Ike liked the sound of the president and his wife talking almost as much as he liked cigars. He made it a point to stand near the couple during their chats, chewing on grass or tobacco. It relaxed him. Like most animals, he could feel when the humans around him were happy, and he wanted to be happy, too.

On this evening, the president was not particularly happy. He was stressed. The war effort was kicking into high gear. The fighting had been going on for over three years already, and he hoped American assistance might help end it soon.

"We're sending 10,000 troops a day to fight," he told his wife as the sun edged beneath the horizon. "We'll have a million boys in Europe in three months' time."

Edith watched the sheep grazing on the lawn, and she thought of the gardeners who were undoubtedly headed for the front lines. The sheep had been her idea. It was a symbolic gesture and little more. The American people were being asked to give up so much—there were rations on food and gas. They were encouraged to buy Liberty Bonds, which paid for the war. Times were tight. How could she host elegant gourmet dinners on expensive plates while others did without? She couldn't imagine it.

"You and I will have to sacrifice, too," she replied. "A shabby lawn is not enough."

"How about the roses?" asked the president. He pointed to Old Ike, who was chewing on the flowers of a nearby bush.

"I'm serious," she said. "The rationing should impact us, too. Perhaps we can have Meatless Mondays?"

The president startled. "And give up my delicious beef?"

"A lot of Americans are losing much more than that," she reminded him. Edith and the president had no children together. She had once birthed a baby, with her first husband, but the child only lived a few days, and she never had another. Edith worried about all of the mothers whose sons would not come home from the fighting. They were risking so much to make the world safe for democracy. She believed in the war, but its cost frightened her.

"I suppose you're right," the president sighed.

"And Wheatless Wednesdays," she added.

President Wilson watched the ram destroying a bush that had flourished since the first Cleveland administration. Ever since the assassination of Archduke Franz Ferdinand, it had felt to him like everything old was being wiped out. Governments were toppling. Borders were being erased and re-drawn. Now, his diet was being upended.

"That's fine, my dear," he nodded.

Old Ike pulled away from the bush and walked toward Mrs. Wilson. A rosebud protruded from his lips as he prepared to eat it. Instead, as he walked by the First Lady, he spotted a discarded cigar butt a few yards away. He dropped the rose and charged off for his treat. The rose fell by Edith's left foot. The president laughed.

"If I am not careful," he observed, "Old Ike will steal you away from me!"

"Not a chance, my love."

Edith bent down to pick up the bud. The flower was still beautiful, even if the ram had crushed half of it in his jaw. She reached for her husband's hand. The sun was nearly gone, but she thought she saw him smile.

3 THE NEGRO

The hedgerow that separated the White House lawn from the carriage house remained intact little more than three weeks. Around that time, a hole developed in the once-thick wall of vegetation. While Old Ike was not the only sheep to eat the bushes that lined the perimeter of the yard, he was the only one to push through the new gap and set off to explore.

Ulysses S. Grant built the carriage house forty-five years earlier. Originally, it held the horse-drawn buggies, which carried the First Family around the city. The twentieth century saw the rise of the automobile, which replaced the buggies. Now, where large-wheeled carriages had sat, there stood a sleek, black Model T Ford.

Old Ike approached the building and, finding the large front doors open, wandered inside. The packed-dirt floor was stained with oil. A variety of tools were spread on workbenches and hanging from hooks on the walls. A lone window allowed a shaft of light to enter the room. There, in the light, sat a lanky, dark-skinned man. His clothes were spotted with grease. His fingernails were caked with grime. He was reading a book.

Keeping a car going in those days took vigilance, and one staff member who had not been given leave to enlist in the army was Clinton Moore, the chauffeur and mechanic. He had wanted to join the fighting, but he had been informed that, if he left, he would not get his job back after the war. The president found him too valuable an employee to lose, he was told.

Clinton wasn't so sure that was the whole story. Washington, D.C., was a Southern city, and President Wilson was a Southern man. Three years earlier, the president had screened the movie "The Birth of a Nation," in which the notoriously violent racists of the Ku Klux Klan were the heroes, saving a white woman from an evil Black man. Wilson had loved the movie. The president called it "history written with lightning." Clinton remembered the Klan differently.

When he was seven years old, his father had purchased a small sheep farm on the outskirts of Lynchburg, Virginia. The Moores were far from wealthy, but they still had more than many poor White farmers in the area. Clinton's father was a skilled breeder, and his flock of Shropshire sheep grew quickly. The first time he gathered wool, he sold it for slightly less than $200, which in those days was a small fortune, and he planned to put aside the money to expand the farm.

That night, Clinton woke up to the sound of a shotgun blast outside his home. Five men on horseback, each wearing a cloth hood to disguise his identity, were outside the door.

"Give us the money!" shouted one. "We know you have it!"

Clinton's father began to protest.

"Shut up, boy!" a second hooded man barked. He leveled his shotgun at Clinton's father. Clinton cried out, he was sure his whole family would be killed.

Instead, his father put his hands high above his head and instructed Clinton's mother to bring the men the bag of money he had placed under his mattress earlier that evening. She did so quickly, as her husband stood, ashamed, on the porch, looking down a gun barrel.

The man with the gun did not lower it until another man counted the money to make sure they were getting the full amount. When they were certain they had taken every last dollar from Mr. Moore's wool sale, they galloped away.

No, the Ku Klux Klan were not heroes. They were thieves and criminals. Clinton's father sold the farm not long after that and moved the family north to the city, where he got a job caring for the horses in the White House stables. Clinton had followed in his footsteps.

Clinton's father advised his son to work hard but to never make a White man feel equal to him. When Whites found themselves equal to Blacks, he had said, there was trouble.

***

On the afternoon that Old Ike entered the carriage house. Clinton was busy reading *The Negro* by W.E.B. Du Bois, which told of the great African heritage that had never been taught to American Blacks. For centuries, slaves and their descendants had been told that Africa was a savage place, full of cannibals and danger. Historians had said that Africans needed Whites to direct them, or they would fall back into savagery.

Of course, White men wrote these histories, and since only White men had been allowed to go to college, the stories got skewed. Du Bois was the first African American to graduate from Harvard, and he made it his mission to correct the kind of awful racism in "The Birth of a Nation" and in history books.

Clinton had always heeded his father's advice. He remembered The Night Riders in their white hoods, and he also remembered the fear he felt that night. But as he read the book, he was also aware of a growing anger inside. He did not like being controlled, and he did not like pretending to feel inferior to anyone, even the president. There had been African kings, after all, men more powerful and respected than a president.

So, engrossed in the book and these feelings, the chauffeur did not see Old Ike approaching. When he finally heard the ram, he startled. This was not a book the president would want him reading during work hours, but as soon as he saw Old Ike, he smiled.

"How'd you get here?" he asked.

He remembered the rams on his father's farm. He knew how to handle them, knew to stay calm and never turn his back. He stood slowly and put his book down. He started patting his pockets, looking for something he could offer the ram, so he could lead him back to the lawn.

He pulled out a handkerchief, some coins, and a few loose cigarettes, setting them down on the workbench. He usually had some sunflower seeds somewhere.

Old Ike turned his head sharply toward the workbench, and at first, Clinton believed that he must have put the seeds with the other items, but a quick look told him this wasn't so. He picked up the coins, wondering if the metallic shine had drawn the ram's eye. Ike didn't pay attention. When Clinton picked up the cigarettes, however, the ram snorted with definite interest.

"Well, I'll be," Clinton whispered to Old Ike. "You're a smoker, aren't you?"

He dropped a cigarette on the floor of the garage and watched the ram devour it. Then, he backed slowly through the open door and across the strip of grass, toward an opening he saw in the hedge.

"Come on, buddy," he coaxed.

Old Ike had already begun to walk toward him, picking up speed when Clinton presented a cigarette to him. Soon, he was charging, his head down.

Clinton tossed the cigarette through the hole and stepped aside just in time for the animal to shoot through, looking for his treat. Clinton hurried back to the carriage house.

"From now on," he thought, "I'll have to keep that door closed."

4 STUCK

August in Washington, D.C., could be miserable. The city had, after all, been built on a swamp. The humid summer air pressed down on the city like a damp blanket, and only the mosquitoes were active. Congress went on recess to escape the heat, leaving the city quieter than normal. This summer, with American troops in French trenches, the president could not go on vacation like the legislators.

Instead, he found himself once again sitting outside with Edith. It had been a relatively quiet summer evening, and the temperature had dropped in the past few days, adding some level of relief to the First Family, who would certainly rather have been at Cape May enjoying the ocean breeze.

Unlike the president and First Lady, the ewes seemed unfazed by the heat. Edith sipped her lemonade and wondered how an animal covered in wool could stand such temperatures. She herself had foregone her usual long sleeves in deference to the weather.

"You know," said her husband, "these beasts do a marvelous job trimming the yard, but they are terribly inconsiderate about their droppings."

"Again, dear? You really must watch your step."

He chuckled. "Truly, truly. My mind has just been elsewhere lately."

"In Amiens?"

The president nodded. The Allied forces (supported by the United States) had begun an assault on German positions in France days before, and they had pushed the enemy back several miles. If they could keep the pressure on, perhaps the war would be over before the year's end. Until this breakthrough, the president's military advisers had assured him that fighting would last well into 1919.

"Perhaps a truce is near?" Edith asked. She did not get the same briefings that the president did, but she was hopeful.

"It seems so," he answered. "And then the next fight begins."

"The next fight?" She was shocked to hear this.

"The fight for peace, my love. Disastrous treaties and mistrust created this catastrophe. We must work together going forward, every country cooperating so the bloodshed ends here."

A sudden clanging startled them. The ewes paced frantically. Something was wrong, and the metallic rattling unnerved everyone further. The president stood and held his hand to his brow, looking for the trouble.

"It's the ram," he said at last.

"Old Ike? What's the matter with him?"

Now the First Lady was standing, too. She had grown fond of the beast, despite his general crankiness and tobacco habit.

The ram came charging into view, skittering in a wild, desperate zig-zag. His head was stuck in a metal pail, and he was unable to see. He shook his head violently—producing the awful ruckus that had disturbed the Wilsons—but the pail stayed put.

Edith moved to help the animal, but her husband waved her back.

"He's too frightened. He might hurt you."

"Woodrow, we cannot let that poor creature suffer more!"

The president thought a moment, and then directed her to the carriage house to fetch the chauffeur, "What's his name, again?"

The First Lady scurried down the driveway, holding her skirts in one hand so they didn't drag on the ground as she ran. By the time she arrived at the carriage house, she found Clinton preparing to leave.

"Thank heavens I've found you!" she yelled. "Do come quickly! We are having a terrible time."

"You want me to bring the car, ma'am?"

"No, no. Just come with me. And hurry!"

When Clinton and Edith arrived, they found Old Ike in a state of high agitation. He was running full-bore from one end of the lawn to the other, turning himself just in time to avoid the hedges. He seemed to be picking up speed as his anxiety increased.

"There you are!" shouted the president. "Can you do something about this?"

His face was pale. He had twice been forced to leap out of the ram's path. One of the wicker chairs was knocked over.

"Mr. President," Clinton spoke slowly, hoping to convey his deepest regrets in a way this powerful man would accept, "I can fix cars just fine, but this is beyond my expertise."

"You aren't good with animals?" the president asked, his brow wrinkled in confusion.

"My father had a farm, sir, but I was just a child when—"

Old Ike stampeded past them, too close to Clinton for comfort.

"—when he sold it and we moved to the city."

"I see," Wilson replied, though he clearly didn't. "So what shall we do about this?"

"I'm not sure, sir."

"We should have kept the gardeners," the president muttered.

The ram had turned and was making another pass. He was headed straight for Mrs. Wilson, who stood, frozen, directly ahead of him.

"Edith!" the president screamed. He was suddenly very afraid.

At the last possible second, the First Lady stepped aside. As Old Ike passed, she brought her fist down solidly on the metal pail, and it slid loose. Ike slowed, then stopped. With a final, hearty shake from left to right, he sent the bucket tumbling to the ground.

"My goodness, Edith! Back away from him!"

The First Lady stood still. The ram was still frightened. He snorted and pawed at the ground. She began to whisper to him.

"You're a good boy," she cooed. "That was very upsetting, but it's all finished now, isn't it? Everything is all better..."

Old Ike began to feel a little more calm. The woman's voice soothed him.

The First Lady looked around at the men and continued to speak gently to the ram. She reached out slowly toward the animal and gently rubbed the rough fur on the ram's broad forehead.

And just like that, Old Ike realized how tired the fuss had made him, and he plopped to the ground for a rest.

The two men were still standing ten feet away, gaping in disbelief.

"Gentlemen," she said, raising her chin high, "never underestimate what a woman can do!"

5 STRESS

As summer gave way to autumn, pleasant temperatures and gentle breezes replaced the stifling heat. Congress returned to the city, and the business of government picked up again.

Old Ike was not concerned about legislation in the autumn of 1918. He wasn't even overly concerned with tobacco. He was focused, as all rams of his breed are during the fall, with mating.

In the wild, rams must compete with each other to prove their strength and win the admiration of the ewes.

Because Ike was the only male in the White House herd, he had no competition, but he still wanted to headbutt something. It was in his nature, after all, and the mating season wasn't complete without some sort of fun.

Inside the White House, the president met with his Secretary of State, Robert Lansing, in the Oval Office. The Allies had pushed the Germans back. The Great War seemed to be ending.

"You'll have to travel, Mr. President," Lansing advised. "When hostilities end, you'll need to go to Europe for the peace talks."

President Wilson leaned back in his chair and ran a hand over his face. "Yes, I suppose you're right." He had never been able to handle stress very well. His blood pressure would rise and he would fall ill. The war had not been good for him, and the delicate task of building a lasting peace would likely take a further toll.

"The idea of a unified governing body, with each country represented—" the Secretary of State began.

"A League of Nations," the president chimed in.

"Yes, that's right—the League of Nations. That will be very difficult to create. You'll have to get all of the other governments to sign on, and then you'll have to get the treaty through Congress."

"Mr. Lansing, I am well aware of the difficulties involved. But I hope you realize, as I do, that without such a pact we cannot prevent another war. All of this carnage means nothing if we do not ensure peace for future generations."

The president was a devout Calvinist, a Christian who believed that every event in life was part of a Divine plan. This terrible war, he thought, was God's way of convincing people to change their ways.

Without the horrors the world had experienced over the last four years, international cooperation might have remained just a far-off dream. Now, even with the obstacles, it was closer than ever.

Secretary Lansing was about to speak when the two men heard shouts in the hallway.

"What the devil is that ruckus?" the president fumed. He was not one who tolerated wild behavior. He rushed to the door and opened it.

His personal secretary was standing on her desk. Old Ike was charging down the hallway, away from the president.

"He came out of nowhere," the terrified woman explained, "and he broke those chairs!" She pointed to a pile of wood that had, until two minutes prior, been a place for visitors to wait for the president.

"Andrew Jackson bought those chairs," the secretary moaned.

"They were never comfortable, anyway," the president sighed. "We'll have to get better ones." He hurried after the animal.

Old Ike made his way into the East Room of the White House. He wanted to head-butt more things. It felt good on his thick skull. It had been no problem to crash through the door that led from the lawn into the Executive building. Since then, he'd been looking for things to destroy.

He looked for something significant to destroy—an old cabinet full of dishes, perhaps, or a fragile writing desk. He continued through various rooms, giving brief charges toward any people he saw. They hurried quickly out of his way.

His nose brought him, finally, to the kitchen, where lunch preparations were underway. The cooks fled when he entered, leaving a tray of ham sandwiches sitting on a wooden island in the center of the room. Ike ambled over, taking a momentary break from his rampage to snatch one of the sandwiches. He was standing by the table eating when the president caught up with him.

"You dirty rascal," President Wilson scolded. "You do not belong in this house, and if you do not remove yourself at once, I will have mutton chops for dinner tonight. Do you hear me?"

The ram did hear the president, but he did not understand English. He grabbed a second sandwich, feeling a little better about his day.

The president moved briskly to a door, which he opened. A cool autumn breeze swept into the room. Old Ike raised his head, still chewing on a mouthful of bread and ham.

"Go on, you scoundrel," the president ordered, motioning toward the outdoors. "Out with you!"

Old Ike looked at the man with a sense of pity. He decided that he would try to smash this person just as soon as he finished his snack.

Just then, a ewe wandered by the open door, unaware of the commotion inside, catching Old Ike's eye. He swallowed the food and trotted through the open door. President Wilson slammed the door shut behind him with relief.

Secretary Lansing arrived. He was relieved to find the Commander-in-Chief unbroken by the wild animal.

"Sir, are you all right?"

"Fine," replied the president. "It seems appropriate that before I travel to Europe to negotiate for our future that I must first shepherd my own house to peace."

6 THE SENATOR

I t was eleven minutes past eleven on the morning of November 11, 1918, when the Great War officially ended. 11:11 on 11/11. More than four years of death ended with the stroke of a clock's arm. The world was no longer on fire, although the ashes were still smoldering.

In the early part of the next year, President Wilson prepared for a trip to Paris, where he would meet with other political leaders to rebuild the world for permanent peace. Wilson was cheerful about the war's end and optimistic about the future.

Not everyone agreed with the president's views on the future. Henry Cabot Lodge, the powerful senator from Massachusetts, believed that the United States should not join forces with European countries, even in the service of peace. After all, he argued, the recent war had happened because of well-intentioned treaties.

On a late November Sunday, the president and his wife traveled to Walter Reed General Hospital to visit wounded men who had returned from the fighting in Europe. Many of these soldiers had lost arms or legs. Some had been blinded. It was difficult to see the devastation of war firsthand, but both of the Wilsons believed it was important for the nation's Commander-in-Chief to visit and thank those who had fought for their country.

Clinton, the chauffeur, had not been invited inside the hospital. He stayed with the car, which gave him plenty of time to think. He had wanted to fight but had not been allowed. As angry as this made him, he also realized that it likely preserved his health. It possibly saved his life.

On the drive back to the Executive Mansion, the president recounted his childhood memories of the Civil War. He had seen death and disgrace firsthand, growing up a child in the South. At one point, he had even seen Confederate President Jefferson Davis paraded through the streets in chains by Union troops.

"We cannot allow this sort of suffering to happen again," he said somberly.

"Truly," replied his wife, who, after the Civil War, had also grown up in the South.

"I think the various heads of state will agree. The trouble is fellows like Lodge. They know nothing of sacrifice or honor. They only understand cowardice and self-preservation. It must be, it seems to me, some sort of Yankee heritage."

"Senator Lodge is a fool," his wife replied, "but I don't see that as a trait exclusive to Northerners."

"My dear, you were not yet born when Sherman marched through the South, burning farms and houses, setting ignorant slaves free to run wild, terrorizing the good people."

Clinton stiffened, but he kept his eyes on the road and his mouth closed. This was not the first time White people had forgotten that he was present and that he could hear them.

"What worries me most is anarchism," the president continued. "Those who hate government will try to take advantage of the current situation in Europe. If they succeed, it will mean chaos. Maybe even Bolshevism."

Clinton turned the Model T into the White House driveway and pulled to a stop by the building's entrance. He hopped out and opened Mrs. Wilson's door. She turned to step out, then paused. Standing twenty feet away, staring at her, was Old Ike. She cleared her throat, met his gaze, and stood up. The ram backed up a few feet.

The White House door banged open and a tall man with a pointed goatee charged out, followed by a flustered secretary.

"Senator Lodge," Edith greeted him coldly.

"Mrs. Wilson," the Senator replied, matching her frigid tone.

"I tried to stop him," the secretary blurted, "but he wouldn't wait, and—"

"It's fine, Miss Carlson," the president assured her as he exited the car. "I'm sure the Senator has something quite urgent to tell me."

The two politicians glared at each other. Neither smiled.

Edith excused herself and went inside with the secretary. This broke the tension enough that Lodge began to speak.

"Mr. President, I am gravely concerned about your plans for negotiation in Paris. You cannot bind us to Europe. The United States must be free to do as it will! We will not be controlled by foreign interests!"

"Due respect, Senator," the president replied, "but as president, it is my duty to negotiate peace, not yours."

"And it is the duty of Congress—" Lodge started. He noticed Clinton standing silently by the car. "Would you kindly leave, sir?" he demanded. "These matters are not for your consideration."

"I understand, Senator," Clinton replied, "but I am employed by the president, not the Congress, so I will await his instruction."

Wilson chuckled, but Lodge's face tensed and reddened. He turned to face the driver.

"Why you impudent cur!" he began.

Lodge had turned his back on Old Ike, who viewed the move as an invitation. The ram lowered his head and bolted forward.

Clinton saw the trouble first, and he grabbed the Senator just in time to pull him out of harm's way. The two men fell to the ground as Old Ike stormed past and ran full-speed into the driver's door of the Model T. The ram stepped back, dazed, and collapsed to the ground.

Clinton helped Senator Lodge to his feet, dusting him off as he did so. Lodge said nothing further to the driver. Instead, he pointed at the unconscious animal.

"A perfect example of your poor judgment," he told the president.

"Funny," Wilson remarked, "but I think I rather like him."

7 SHEARING

The president and Mrs. Wilson set off for Europe, headed to the palace at Versailles where the terms of peace would be negotiated. President Woodrow Wilson was hopeful that he could leverage America's decisive role in ending the war into the kind of peace treaty he wanted, something with broad, international cooperation to prevent anything like the Great War from ever happening again.

Edith, with whom the president discussed almost all of his policy decisions, went along. He could bounce ideas off her, vent about the other leaders, or simply relax in her company.

In their absence, the White House ran on a skeleton crew. The Executive Mansion was relatively quiet, aside from the tourists who stopped by to gawk at the building. No sitting president had ever left the country before. The building had never been empty for so long.

Clinton spent most of his days hiding out in the garage with a book. There wasn't much pressure to do actual work with the Wilsons in Europe. After the ram damaged the Model T Ford, the president had requested a new car, a Pierce-Arrow. The change in vehicle meant that Clinton had to gain familiarity with a new transmission and a new feel for driving. The president's absence was an ideal time to practice. He took the car out when he could, but he always asked one of the White staff members to accompany him, sitting in the back seat. He did not want an over-zealous policeman to think he had stolen the vehicle.

In early May of 1919, it was time to shear the flock of sheep, and Clinton was ordered to leave the Pierce-Arrow in the garage and help collect wool. He remembered helping his father at shearing time, but he had been so young then that he had not been much involved. He was glad to find that he would not be responsible for using the shears—two farmers had been hired to do that.

Clinton was expected to herd the unshorn animals into pens and assist in other ways as needed.

One of the biggest concerns in shearing is keeping the sheep still while the wool is removed. If a sheep tries to run off during the process, they could be cut accidentally. For this reason, most farmers turn the sheep upside down during the cutting. It keeps the animal in place, and it allows the shearer easy access to the wool.

For most of the afternoon, Clinton stood by the pen, allowing one ewe at a time out for shearing. The farmers would grab the sheep and flip it over, working busily with their shears to clip the wool. After the ewe was shorn, she would be released to the lawn, where she could resume her grazing.

The men had decided to save Old Ike for last, feeling that it was better to contain him so he did not cause problems during the wool collection. This tactic worked well at first, but as the afternoon progressed, Clinton noticed that the ram was increasingly agitated. Ike stalked the perimeter of the pen, rubbing his horns on the bars and stomping his feet. By the time the last ewe was clean-shaven, Old Ike was downright furious. When the men approached the pen to shear him, he charged and rammed his head into the wall as a warning.

"Maybe we should leave him alone," one of the farmers said. "We got the rest of them."

"Due respect, sir," Clinton interjected, "but that might kill him."

Flies, he knew, will lay eggs in wool if it is left on sheep. The eggs then became maggots, which could kill a sheep.

"He might kill us, though," the farmer replied.

Clinton thought back to his childhood, looking for tricks that his father had used to soothe angry animals, but he couldn't remember any. Their time as farmers had been so short.

The farmer pulled out a small pouch of chewing tobacco. He reached inside, pinched a small amount between his thumb and index finger, and shoved it into his mouth, next to teeth already stained by the practice. Clinton had an idea.

"Can I have your tobacco?" he asked the man.

"Boy, I'm not running a charity."

"It's not for me," Clinton protested. He pointed at Old Ike. "It's for him."

The farmer stared in disbelief at the agitated animal. He handed his pouch to Clinton. The chauffeur whistled to get Old Ike's attention. Once he had it, he waved the tobacco pouch in the air and then dropped it inside the pen.

"All of it?" the farmer protested. He had paid twenty-five cents for that package.

Old Ike ran forward and began gnawing on the pouch, taking the dried and shredded leaves of tobacco into his mouth. He chewed heartily, brown globs of saliva hanging from his mouth. The sight disgusted Clinton, but he could see the ram relaxing with each chew. The nicotine was soothing the beast. Finally, Old Ike swallowed his chaw and sat down, satisfied.

"Now, you can shear him," Clinton told the farmer.

"Well, I'll be," the man replied. "That's the darnedest thing I've ever seen!"

Within minutes, Old Ike's wool was off, and he was grazing on the south lawn of the White House again.

The wool from the White House sheep was packaged and cleaned, then taken to auction. Old Ike's wool sold for $10,000 a pound, a price that to this day is the highest ever paid. As the president had promised, the money was donated to the Red Cross. The ram had done his part in the war effort.

8 MISFORTUNE

In late September of 1919, the president—recently back from Europe—decided to undertake a whistle-stop train tour in support of the League of Nations. He and his wife moved into a train car called the Mayflower and set off through the country. It was not a pleasant way to travel.

Trains of that time had no air-conditioning. Windows could be opened, of course, but hot air could not be cooled. As the president's car traveled through Colorado, it passed near a wildfire, filling the train with smoke. The windows were shut. The outside temperatures in that part of the country spiked at more than 100° Fahrenheit, and an enclosed train full of people was no doubt even hotter.

It's hard to say if what happened next was caused by the heat or by the stress of events, but the president suffered a stroke on that trip. He had bleeding in his brain that paralyzed the left side of his body and his speech became incoherent. The remainder of the tour was canceled and the First Family returned to Washington, D.C.

Edith spent most of the following days at her husband's bedside, but she still came outside in the evenings to see the sunset and have time for herself. Her first husband had died years ago. She was heartbroken at the thought that her second husband was so ill. The doctors told her that he was quite near death. Rest, they said, was the only cure for his sickness.

The sheep still grazed the White House lawn. Troops had started to return to the United States from their duties in Europe, but by now the animals who had been acquired to help with the landscaping while the men were away felt like part of the scenery at the Executive Mansion.

Lambs now tottered among the older sheep, all of them owing their existence to Old Ike. Visitors would stop at the fence along Pennsylvania Avenue and watch them scamper and play. Ike had become quite good at badgering these visitors for tobacco, and every day he ate at least two cigars.

Edith observed all of this, grateful for some reminder of a normal life in her fractured world. She and the president had only been married three years, but their connection was deep. It pained her to see him in bed, barely able to communicate. He was a great man brought low by sickness. She worried that his plans for peace would also suffer.

Without him out front, making speeches, would the American people understand the importance of the League of Nations? Fools like Henry Cabot Lodge still made speeches, filling the silence left by her husband.

She had to nurse her husband back to health. The country—perhaps even the world—needed Woodrow Wilson now. But how was he to rest in a job as stressful and demanding as the presidency? There were papers to read, bills to sign, decisions to make, dignitaries to greet. Her husband's responsibilities were constant. Presidents are never truly on vacation, even when they say they are.

As far as Edith could tell, she had two options. She could go public with the extent of her husband's illness, which could lead to a national crisis as Congress argued over his fitness to be president, but such a struggle would undermine America's newfound role as a world power, and it could kill the League of Nations.

Or, perhaps, she could try to avoid that by protecting the president from outsiders. He was sick. With rest, he would hopefully get better and be able to resume his full workload. All she needed to do was buy some time. How much time, she wasn't sure.

Across the expanse of grass, she spotted Old Ike. She remembered how the ram had chased the reporter over the hedge during the president's press conference about the White House sheep. She had also heard about the near-miss with Senator Lodge. If only that chauffeur hadn't pulled Lodge out of the way. She would have loved to see that dandy from Massachusetts running for his life. She smiled at the thought.

"I may need your help, Old Ike," she said to herself. The ram looked over at her, his mouth full of tobacco. For a second, she was certain that he nodded.

9 THE EXECUTIVE

Edith worked day and night protecting her husband. As paperwork arrived on his desk, she read and studied it. The best way she could help Woodrow was to shield him from any unnecessary burden.

Visitors were the easiest to deal with. The president had not left his bed in weeks. He no longer shaved. Turning away visiting congressmen or foreign leaders was not a problem for her. Edith was firm, and the guest in question rarely persisted once she said no. Only doctors could see the president, and even then she was selective, allowing only those who could be trusted.

She also had to handle her husband's mail. Anything that did not require an official response was discarded. If a pressing matter could be passed along to one of her husband's Cabinet members to be handled, she would do so. Only when an item required the direct involvement of the president did she share it with her husband. Even then, he was not able to sign his own papers, so she would forge his signature. She did not like doing it, but it had to be done. The other option was allowing all of the president's work to be undone by Republicans in the Senate. She felt the vice president was not capable enough to push through Wilson's agenda. Henry Cabot Lodge would destroy him. Edith had to prevent that.

In the early 20th century, the press tended to accept the word of the president's doctors without attempting to dig deeper. And so, Edith Wilson was able to protect her husband for several months. The public knew that the president was sick—very sick. He had not given speeches or even appeared in public for months. What they did not know—what only Wilson's enemies guessed at—was that the First Lady was actually running the Executive Branch of the government.

During all of this, the Senate was debating whether the United States should join the League of Nations. The Democrats—the president's party—held a majority, but they did not control the two-thirds needed to approve a treaty. Standing in the way of the League was Henry Cabot Lodge.

Lodge had told his friends that he hated President Wilson, and he made it his mission to block the president's policies. He did not want the country to join the League, because he feared the Treaty gave too much power to the president and not enough to Congress.

Under normal circumstances, President Wilson would probably have met with Lodge and worked toward a compromise. Or, perhaps, he would have given speeches to rally the public against Lodge. Now, with his left side paralyzed, on doctors' orders to rest, Wilson could not fight back. These were not normal circumstances.

Just how unusual things had gotten was becoming a matter of public concern. President Wilson had not been seen in public for months. Rumors were spreading that he was near death. Some people even began to whisper that he had died and that Edith was hiding the truth. She knew that the public must see the president in order to disprove these rumors.

On a warm spring day in 1920, Edith shaved her husband's scraggly white beard and helped him get dressed. He was transferred from his bed into a wheelchair and taken outside. President Wilson squinted his eyes against the sun and looked around at the White House lawn.

Cheers went up from the tourists who had been standing by the black metal fence that guarded the lawn's perimeter. Wilson was popular among the American people, who had rallied around him in wartime and had since been greatly concerned about his health. The president raised his right hand and waved at the crowd. The right corner of his lip turned up in a smile.

"Edith," he said to his wife, "we are fortunate." His voice was low and weak.

"Yes," she replied through tears. "We certainly are."

Old Ike, upon hearing the president's voice, trotted over to the couple and sat at the Commander-in-Chief's feet. He looked up at Wilson, his dark eyes searching the man's face.

"Hi there, Old Ike." The president reached his right hand down toward the ram.

"He missed you," Edith noted. "Everyone has."

"I know, my dear. I know."

The president tried to lean down to better pet Old Ike, but the effort was too great, and he soon collapsed back against the seat.

Edith understood that her husband would never be his old self again. Whatever improvements he would make in the coming months, they would never restore him to the man he had been. She wanted to weep, but she knew she had to be strong for him.

The election of 1920 was approaching, and the First Lady knew her husband should not seek a third term. She was glad to know her time as the country's chief (if secret) decision-maker was almost over.

The White House gate opened, and a long, black McFarlan limousine pulled into the driveway. It approached the Wilsons and stopped twenty feet away. A window rolled down. Senator Lodge stuck his head through the window.

"Mister President," he called, "I've been trying to meet with you but have not been allowed."

"Here I am," said the president.

Lodge waved his hand at Old Ike, "I shall not leave my car while that horrific beast is near. Can you have him put away?"

"Certainly not," Wilson replied.

Old Ike stood up, eyeing the Senator.

"Senator Lodge," said Edith, "do please be brief. My husband needs rest."

"Unlike your husband, the affairs of our great nation do not rest," the Senator replied. "We must discuss the Treaty of Versailles. I cannot support it as written, and until it is approved, we remain at war with Germany and Austria."

Old Ike stood and approached the car, his snout raised high, his nostrils flaring. Lodge leaned back from the window just a little.

"Then I suggest you support the Treaty and urge your fellow Republicans to join you," President Wilson called. His anger was rising. Edith rose to push his wheelchair inside.

"I'm not through," cried Lodge. "Don't you walk away!"

Old Ike could see his reflection in the black shiny paint of Lodge's car. The ram lowered his head so that he was in perfect head-butting position. He snorted and pawed at the ground with his hoof, a gesture of intimidation.

"Oh no you don't," Lodge cried out, furiously trying to roll up his window before driving away. Old Ike charged down the lane after the car.

"You have your answer, Senator," Edith called after the car.

As the car pulled out of the ground's gate, Old Ike stopped charging but carried on bleating for quite some time. He sounded just like a man taunting and laughing, Edith delighted in noting.

"That Old Ike is a funny old thing," she said to her husband as she turned to roll him into the White House.

"That he is, love. That he is."

EPILOGUE

Despite his ill health, Woodrow Wilson did seek a third term in 1920. The delegates of the Democratic National Convention, however, were afraid that the President was too ill to campaign, and they nominated Ohio Governor James Cox instead. Cox promised to fight for the League of Nations.

On November 2, 1920, Cox lost in a landslide to fellow Ohioan, Senator Warren G. Harding. Harding had run on his opposition to the United States joining the League of Nations. President Wilson's dream of a world united in peace slipped away.

In the months between the election and the inauguration—which in those days was March 4—much had to be done. Personal belongings needed to be packed. New living arrangements had to be made. The sheep which lived on the lawn had to go, too.

It was decided that Old Ike and the rest of the flock—which, thanks to the ram, had grown to seventy—would move to the Maryland farm of L. C. Probert. Fortunately for Old Ike, Probert was a cigar smoker, and the animal's addiction to tobacco would be satisfied daily.

Woodrow Wilson rode to the inauguration with President-Elect Harding in his Pierce-Arrow, and, after the ceremony, he left for a townhouse in another part of the city. He and his wife took daily drives in the car, but not with Clinton Moore, who stayed on at the White House during the Harding Administration.

President Wilson died at home on February 3, 1924. Edith lived for another 37 years, dying on December 28, 1961. It was Woodrow Wilson's birthday.

Old Ike outlived the President by a little more than a year. He died happily, chewing on a cigar that Probert had given him. His life had been eventful, and his place in history as assured. Old Ike was a cantankerous beast, but few other animals have so faithfully served a President.

Historical Figures & Events

This book is a work of historical fiction. Many of the characters are real, and the historical events they discuss are as well. However, wide latitude was taken during the writing of this book in an attempt to combine the story of Old Ike with the important people and happenings of his times. Some characters—most notably Clinton Moore, the chauffeur—are entirely fictional.

Below are some of the real figures and events that helped shape this story.

OLD IKE

Yes, the ram chewed tobacco and lived at the White House. He was not, by any accounts, friendly. Most rams aren't. His wool did sell for $10,000 a pound, though, and that makes up for a lot of shortcomings.

WOODROW WILSON

The 28th President of the United States was an idealistic man who believed that world cooperation would prevent future war. He was dedicated to the idea of the League of Nations, and he was touring the country by train in support of the League when a stroke brought him down. Had he not fallen so ill, the US might have joined the League. Whether this could have prevented World War II is subject to debate.

Wilson's racist views of African-Americans (then called Negros) are well-documented. He was a Southern man, and his ideas fit with the predominant views of the South at that time. That a person can be so admirable in some areas and so asinine in others is a problem any student of history grapples with regularly.

EDITH WILSON

Edith Bolling Wilson led a fascinating life before she met President Wilson. She was a woman with only two years of formal education, but after her first husband's death, she ran his business successfully. She bought an electric car, and she was the first woman to receive a driver's license in the District of Colombia.

She met the recently widowed Woodrow Wilson in 1915. They married the next year. She remained devoted to him for the rest of his life and devoted to his legacy after that. She was not our first official female president, but she did determine what matters came to the President's attention after his stroke. Very few people have impacted a presidency as she did.

HENRY CABOT LODGE

The senator from Massachusetts was Wilson's toughest adversary in Congress, and he was never more powerful than when he blocked US entry into the League of Nations. He was a friend of President Theodore Roosevelt, and it was Roosevelt to whom he confided his personal hatred for President Wilson.

THE BIRTH OF A NATION

D. W. Griffith's film is a landmark in cinematic history. It pioneered a variety of film techniques and has been a stylistic influence on almost every film since. The film is also unrepentantly racist, showing former slaves as ignorant at best and a threat to White womanhood at worst. While President Wilson's love for the film was not uncommon—in fact, the film was a major hit—there were protests and objections at the time, most notably by the National Association for the Advancement of Colored People (NAACP).

W.E.B. DU BOIS

Dr. Du Bois was perhaps the leading African-American intellectual of his time. He is best known for his long-running oversight of the NAACP's newsletter, *The Crisis*, and his classic book *The Souls of Black Folk*.

THE KU KLUX KLAN

Founded in the aftermath of the Civil War, the Klan is a White Christian terrorist organization. In its first incarnation, it terrorized Blacks and federal employees in the South during Reconstruction. When Reconstruction ended, the Klan petered out.

After *The Birth of a Nation*, the Klan was reborn nationwide and enjoyed a period of power during the early 1920s. Later, during the civil rights movement of the 1950s and 1960s, they were a constant threat to the lives of protestors and political activists. Members of the

KKK killed three civil rights workers in Philadelphia, Mississippi, in 1964. The modern KKK preaches White supremacy, opposes immigration, denounces Jews and Catholics, and commits acts of vandalism and violence to express these odious opinions.

WORLD WAR I

In 1914, Archduke Franz Ferdinand was assassinated during a visit to Sarajevo, setting off a cataclysmic chain of events that resulted in a war between the major European powers. Millions died. Millions more suffered.

A large part of the fighting took place in trenches—large ditches dug into the battlefield and fortified with machine guns. Battles were fought for control over surprisingly small pieces of territory. The British and French fought the Germans, as they would again two decades later. How many American boys would die in foreign trenches before the fighting ended? 117,465 Americans died during the war, though not all were in trenches.

THE CIVIL WAR

The Civil War was a struggle between Southern states, which wanted to form a new country, and Northern states, which refused to accept the South's plans to leave. The key issue that sparked the war was slavery. The South's economy was based on selling cotton planted and harvested using slave labor. In the North, there was no need for slavery because the economy was based on manufacturing. Many Northerners were opposed to slavery, which Southerners felt was unfair and hypocritical. After the election of Abraham Lincoln in 1860, many Southern states decided to leave the United States and form their own country, the Confederate States of America. Jefferson Davis was the Head of the Confederate States of America.

THE TREATY OF VERSAILLES

The Treaty was named after the massive palace constructed by French King Louis XIV, which was used for meetings between the major powers as they determined the terms of peace. Because Germany lost the war, it was punished severely by the terms of the treaty. Germany was forced to pay other nations for damages suffered during the war. This effectively destroyed the German economy, building resentment that eventually made it possible for Adolf Hitler to gain power. In essence, the Treaty bears a great deal of responsibility for World War II.

THE LEAGUE OF NATIONS

This international body was designed to prevent war from ever happening again. President Wilson was a major supporter of the idea, but his stroke undermined efforts to have the United States join the League. Without US participation, the League was unable to prevent World War II.

WARREN G. HARDING

Elected to follow Wilson as President, Warren Harding took a much more isolated view of foreign policy and did not impose regulations on businesses. When he died in 1923, two years into his presidency, he was quite popular. Shortly afterwards, scandals involving his Cabinet members changed public opinion. Most historians now rank him as one of the country's worst presidents.

Glossary

AMIENS: site of a major battle during World War I

ANARCHISM: the political belief that governments are, by nature, cruel and tyrannical. (In the early 20th century, anarchists were considered a major threat to the United States. An anarchist assassinated President William McKinley in 1901.)

BILL: a piece of proposed legislation that, if passed by Congress and signed by the president, becomes a law

BOLSHEVISM: the Russian form of communism, an economic theory where the government controls property

CABINET MEMBER: key advisor to the president

CAPE MAY: a resort town in New Jersey

CHAW: a chew of tobacco

CONGRESS: the legislative branch of the US government, made up of the House of Representatives and the Senate

CUR: a mixed-breed dog, or a person with no social standing

THE EAST ROOM: the largest room in the White House, used for receptions and banquets

THE FIRST FAMILY: comprised of the president, the president's spouse, and their children (And their pets, too!)

LIBERTY BONDS: a loan to the government to support the war effort that the government promised to repay with interest after the war was over

McFARLAIN LIMO: a premium car company, now defunct

MODEL T FORD: the first mass-produced car, cheap enough to be purchased by most Americans

PIERCE ARROW: a luxury car

THE RED CROSS: a humanitarian organization that provides disaster relief and emergency assistance

SECRETARY OF STATE: the presidential advisor responsible for handling America's official interactions with other nations (Robert Lansing was the Secretary of State from 1915-1920.)

STROKE: poor blood flow to the brain resulting in cell death causing part of the brain to stop working (Strokes can be fatal.)

YANKEE: slang for a Northerner

WHISTLESTOP TRAIN TOUR: when politicians traveled by train and spoke to crowds at train stations in the days before TV or radio

Further Reading

For more information on Edith Wilson's role in her husband's administration, read *Madam President* by William Hazelgrove. Most of the factually correct information in this book came to the author from that source.

To learn more about the violence and deprivation facing African Americans in the early part of the 20th century, read *At the Hands of Persons Unknown: The Lynching of Black America*, by Philip Dray. It is a devastating look at one of the worst segments of American history.

The classic book about World War I is *The Guns of August*, by Barbara Tuchman.

ABOUT THE AUTHOR

Andrew Hager, graduated from Towson University in 2003 with an undergraduate degree in Political Science. After obtaining a Master of Arts in Teaching (also from Towson) in 2006, he spent a decade teaching Social Studies, Language Arts, and Reading to middle school students for Baltimore County Public Schools in Maryland.

Andrew lives in Lutherville, MD, with his wife and two kids. He travels with his guide dog Sammy, a Labrador Retriever trained to assist the blind. You can reach Andrew through his email at: historian@presidentialpetmuseum.com

ABOUT THE ILLUSTRATOR

A mild-mannered librarian by day, Nora Sawyer spends her nights reading stories and drawing pictures. She lives on a boat with her husband and a ridiculous dog just north of San Francisco, CA.

ABOUT THE PRESIDENTIAL PET MUSEUM

 The Presidential Pet Museum is the world's largest collection of information and artifacts related to those animals who have called the White House home. Founded by Claire McLean, the Museum is the recognized authority on presidential pet history, referenced in articles by The New York Times, AOL News, Newsweek, The Economist and other outlets.

In January 2017, Bill "WooFDriver" Helman became director of the Museum. Bill is working to expand the museum's outreach to schools, libraries, and on social media. The POTUS PETS series is one such innovation.

ABOUT THE DIRECTOR OF THE MUSEUM

Bill "WoofDriver" Helman, has over twenty years of experience as an urban dog musher and adventurer. As an animal advocate with a deep interest in history, he is uniquely qualified to act as Director of The Presidential Pet Museum. In this role, Bill wishes to acknowledge and honor the First Pets of the United States who, in large and small ways, influenced the presidential families living in our nation's capital. Bill's goal is to share this distinct and fun facet of American history with the wider public. To learn more about Bill's advocacy work with animals and urban mushing adventures go to www.billhelman.com.

CPSIA information can be obtained
at www.ICGtesting.com
Printed in the USA
LVOW07s1804161017
552627LV00013B/1575/P